Copyright © 2011 Hallmark Licensing, LLC

Published by Hallmark Gift Books, a division of
Hallmark Cards, Inc., Kansas City, MO 64141

All rights reserved. No part of this publication may
be reproduced, transmitted, or stored in any form
or by any means without the prior written permission
of the publisher.

Editor: Emily Osborn
Art Director: Kevin Swanson
Designer: Mary Eakin
Production Artist: Dan Horton

Photo Stylist: Betsy Gantt Stewart
Set Builder: Randy Stewart
Photo Retoucher: Greg Ham
Project Coordinator: Becky Jaques
Photographer: Jake Johnson
Storyboard & Character Development: Karla Taylor
Character & Prop Designers: Ken Crow, Ruth Donikowski,
Rich Gilson, and Susan Tague

ISBN: 978-1-59530-895-0
SKU: XKT4000

Printed and bound in China
JUN13

A Gift For

_____

From

_____

Dedicated to the students
and staff of Metzler Elementary.
Go Huskies!
-T.S.Z.

How to Use Your Interactive Story Buddy®

1. Activate your Story Buddy by pressing the "On / Off" button on the ear.
2. Read the story aloud in a quiet place. Speak in a clear voice when you see the highlighted phrases.
3. Listen to your Story Buddy respond with several different phrases throughout the book.

Clarity and speed of reading affect the way Jingle® responds. He may not always respond to young children.

Watch for even more Interactive Story Buddy characters. For more information, visit us on the Web at Hallmark.com/StoryBuddy.

I Reply TECHNOLOGY®

Hallmark's **I Reply Technology** brings your Story Buddy® to life! When you read the key phrases out loud, your Story Buddy gives a variety of responses, so each time you read feels as magical as the first.

BOOK 2

A Snow Day for Jingle

By Tom Shay-Zapien

Hallmark

There are four seasons in each and every year,
but wintertime was Jingle's favorite. The thought of
sledding, romping through the snow, and catching icy
flakes on his tongue made Jingle want to sing!

But while the frosty air outside made it *feel* like wintertime, it certainly didn't *look* like wintertime in Pineville. Not a single snowflake had fallen from the sky. Jingle tried to guess just how long it would take for the first snowfall to arrive.

Five minutes?

Five hours?

Five days?

Jingle quickly realized he'd have to wait patiently. After all, that is what good dogs do and Jingle was a good dog.

Jingle decided spending some time at school would help take his mind off how much it wasn't snowing. So he followed Andrew to the bus stop.

"You know I can't take you to school, buddy," said Andrew. "When I get home, we can play together . . . I promise. Sorry, Jingle . . . you've gotta go home."

The next morning when Jingle woke up, he looked out the window. Then he eagerly nudged Andrew's cheek. Peeking out his window, Andrew quickly realized what Jingle was trying to tell him. "Wow!" shouted Andrew. "Look at all that snow!"

Pineville was covered in a thick white blanket as far as they could see! Andrew gasped. "SNOW DAY!" This made Jingle very happy.

The new-fallen snow crunched beneath their footsteps as Andrew and Jingle plodded happily toward Pineville Park.

A massive plow pushed the sparkling powder aside with ease as it cleared the neighborhood streets. Andrew knelt beside Jingle just before the truck rumbled past them. He said, "Jingle, stay." And Jingle did.

Kevin and Jennifer met Andrew and Jingle at the top of the biggest hill in the park. "Race you to the bottom!" shouted Jennifer, holding on to her fluffy cat, Mittens.

"Don't make us wait too long!" chuckled Andrew.

All three laughed out loud as they sped down the snowy slope. Jingle chomped at the falling snowflakes as he and Andrew zipped past everyone else.

Sarah and Jonathan were busy building snowmen at the bottom of the hill when they spotted Andrew and the others. "Hey, guys! Over here!" Jonathan called out. "Come help us finish up!"

Jingle fetched sticks while Andrew, Jennifer, and Kevin decorated the snowmen. Surrounded by his friends, Jingle felt very happy.

The children gazed up at the sky as frosty fluff swirled and twirled downward. The first snow of the season had truly been worth the wait!

"I got one!" shouted Andrew.

"So did I!" Sarah called out with a smile.

Jingle barked with delight.

"Hey!" Kevin said. "Jingle caught one, too! Jingle, you're such a good dog!"

"Has anyone seen Mittens?" asked Jennifer, peeking inside a nearby snow fort. "She was here just a minute ago, but I don't see her anywhere now."

"Maybe she snuck off while we were catching snowflakes," said Jonathan. "I bet we can find her if we split up!"

Before they could even divide up into search
parties, Jingle was eagerly chasing down a long trail
of snowy paw prints.

"This way, guys!" shouted Andrew. "I think
Jingle's found something!"

The tracks led everyone to a tall tree. Stuck in its branches was a winter hat, and playing with the hat was Mittens, just as happy as could be. "Silly cat!" smiled Jennifer, as Mittens plopped down from a low branch and into her arms. "What am I going to do with you?"

"Jingle! You did it!" said Andrew. "You found her kitten!" This made Jingle want to sing!

A reporter from *The Pineville Post,* who was busy snapping photographs of children making snow angels, overheard all the commotion about the lost cat. She also spied Jingle dashing through the snow, headed right to Mittens. "What a heroic little husky pup," she said to herself. Making her way toward the rosy-cheeked crew, she shouted, "Hey, kids! Mind if I take a few pictures for the paper?"

Standing shoulder to shoulder, the kids practiced smiling
for the camera. Andrew patted his puppy's head. "Jingle, stay."
And Jingle did.

As the sun began to set and the crowd at the park began to thin out, Andrew said goodbye to his friends. "Thanks so much for finding Mittens!" said Jennifer.

"This was the best snow day ever!" said Sarah, bouncing in her boots. "See you later! Jingle, I've gotta go home."

"Don't worry, pal," said Andrew softly. "We've got the whole weekend ahead of us. That's two more snow days *just* for you and me." As dog-tired as he was, Jingle felt very happy.

Did you have fun with Jingle® and Andrew?
We would love to hear from you!

Please send your comments to:
Hallmark Book Feedback
P.O. Box 419034
Mail Drop 215
Kansas City, MO 64141

Or e-mail us at:
booknotes@hallmark.com